The world was dark. Without light, the animals couldn't hunt or even see their children.

King Lion called to the animals, "Who will go to the king of the sky and ask for light?"

Eagle screamed, "Me! I can fly the highest."
Off he went into the clouds. But Eagle could not fly
high enough.

Monkey chattered, "Me! I can climb into the sky."
Off he went into the trees. But Monkey could not climb
high enough.

"Me!" boomed Elephant.
"Me!" "Me!" "Me!" called all of the big animals. But they all failed.

Finally Anansi the Spider came forward. "Me! I can spin a web into the sky."

"You?" laughed King Lion. "No, Anansi, you're too little."

"I may be tiny," Anansi replied, "but my friends and I can do anything if we work together."

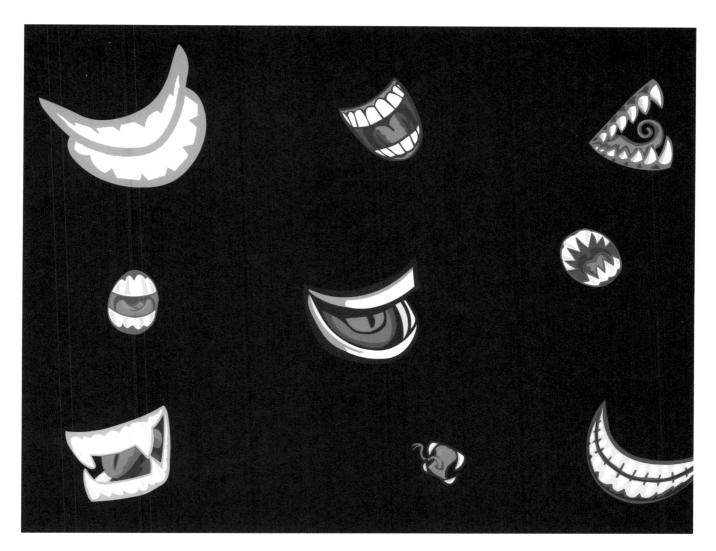

"Ha ha! Hee hee hee! Ho-ho-ho!" the animals laughed. But King Lion roared, "Enough! We shall see what Anansi and his friends can do."

Anansi called out, "Ant! Fly! Let's go."
Anansi began to weave a web from the earth. Sssss! Sssss!
Sssss! It stretched high into the clouds.

"Ant! You and I will climb up the web, and Fly will join us. You can bite an opening into the sky kingdom," explained Anansi. Up they went—chicka-boom, chicka-boom, chicka-boom—until they reached the clouds.

Crunch! Ant chewed an opening in the clouds, and the three friends crawled into the sky kingdom. They were surrounded by bright light and beautiful colors.

Suddenly, the king of the sky stood in front of them.
"What do you want here?" the king demanded.

"We have come for light, King," said Anansi. "Will you please share it with the earth below?"

"We will share," said the king, "but you must prove that you are worthy. You must first pass three tests."
"We can pass any test," bragged Anansi. "Tell us what to do."

"Wait here," said the king. "My wise men and I will prepare the tests."
The king and his wise men went into a golden tent.

"Oh, how I wish I could be a fly on the wall of that tent,"
said Anansi.
"I *can* be a fly on the wall!" buzzed Fly, and he zipped into
the tent to listen.

"They will ask us to cut down every blade of grass in that huge field over there before sunrise tomorrow," Fly cried when he came out.

Fly showed them an area the size of a football field. "It's impossible! We're doomed!" cried Fly.
"Well, the three of us can't do it, but Ant's family can," Anansi said.

"Yes! My family can cut down every blade," Ant yelled, and he ran down Anansi's web to get his mother and his father and his 77 sisters and 82 brothers and all of his cousins and aunts and uncles.

Chomp! Chomp! Crunch-crunch-crunch! Every blade of grass was cut and all of the ants had slid back down the web when the sun came up the next day.

"Humph!" the king huffed. "Well, that was the easiest test.
We shall prepare the next task."
Again, Fly followed the king and his wise men into the tent.

Soon Fly zoomed back out.
"Oh, nooooooooooo!" he moaned. "We must eat all of the fruit on the trees in the orchard between sunset tonight and sunrise tomorrow."

Fly showed them a thousand fruit trees.
"We're doomed!" Ant moaned.

"The three of us can't do it, but Fly's family surely can,"
Anansi said. "Go invite them to a feast."
Fly zipped down to Earth and brought his hungry family to
the orchard.

Thousands of flies swarmed into the trees and began to eat. Bzzzz! Sluuurp! Bzzzzzzzz! Sluuurp! Bzzzzzzzzzz!

The king was furious when he saw the empty fruit trees.
"You must still pass our last test," he bellowed.

Again, Fly became a fly on the wall.
He hurried out to buzz into Anansi's ear, "Choose the gray box," just as the king and his wise men carried two boxes out of the tent.

"This is the final test," said the king. "There is light in one of these boxes. If you choose correctly, it is yours." He held out a small gray box and a huge yellow one. Anansi looked at the boxes. He sniffed them. He turned them and shook them.

Anansi pointed to the gray box. "This box!" he yelled.
The king was enraged. "Take it and go!" he shouted.
Anansi, Ant, and Fly grabbed the box and rushed
down the web.

When they reached the earth, King Lion lifted the top off the box. Nothing but a rooster came out.
Then the rooster puffed out his chest and crowed.

"Er-er-er-er-oooooooooo!"
For the first time, the sun rose brightly into the sky!
Anansi, Ant, and Fly said proudly, "When we work together, we can do anything."